ZAHRA'S CHRISTMAS WISH

DAVEY J. ASHFIELD

Illustrations by Terry Greenwell

For:

Mrs Ashfield,
the best Early Years Teacher in the world

Zahra came to live in our country
and Tommy was her only friend.

Tommy was a metal statue of a soldier.

But Zahra pretended he was alive.

It was Christmas Eve and Zahra danced in the snow.

She sat down and looked in Tommy's sad and weary face.

Zahra was sad too and read her Santa letter to Tommy.

"Dear Santa, my Daddy is far away and frightened.

All I want for Christmas is Daddy to come home."

Then a magical thing happened.

Tommy woke up and he winked his eye at her.

He said, "Don't be sad, Zahra.
Many years ago on Christmas Eve in a war I was frightened.

But a magic Christmas star appeared in the sky and we stopped fighting each other.

Then a magical thing happened.

Tommy woke up and he winked his eye at her.

He said, "Don't be sad, Zahra.
Many years ago on Christmas Eve in a war I was frightened.

But a magic Christmas star appeared in the sky and we stopped fighting each other.

....and we played football."

"We sang a Christmas carol called Silent Night.

Do you know the words Zahra?"

Zahra was so happy her new teacher
had taught her the carol.

She sang.

"Silent night, Holy night.
All is calm, all is bright."

Tommy loved hearing the song again.

Later he told Zahra about the war.

"Sadly, after Christmas we began fighting again and I never came home to my family.

Now people place red poppies on me to remind everyone how horrid war is and to remember soldiers who keep us safe."

Then Tommy smiled and he told Zahra, "Tonight the magic Christmas star may bring your daddy home."

And Tommy told Zahra his own Christmas Wish.

Then a bright star shone over the stormy sea.

Zahra shouted with joy.
"Look Tommy, your magic Christmas Star!"

But the light was from a sinking ship.

Zahra was certain her Daddy was on the ship
and she shouted.
"We must rescue Daddy Tommy!"

"PHEW!"

Tommy blew his football whistle.

He woke up three statues of coal miners.

They ran to save the ship.

Tommy whistled again 'PHEW!'

The metal statue of a lifeboat captain woke up.
The miners sailed with the lifeboat to save the ship.
Zahra stayed to guide the lifeboat back
with a miners' lamp.

Tommy pushed the sinking ship off the rocks and
the lifeboat brought the rescued the sailors
back to Zahra.

But Tommy was sad because he must go back to sleep.

And he did not get his Christmas Wish.

The rescued sailors took photos and videos of Zahra.
"You will be a famous little girl," the Captain said.

But Zahra's daddy wasn't on the ship.

So she was very sad.

And she cried when the wind blew her Santa letter across the sea before she could post it.

Back home her mum and grumpy brother didn't believe her story.

Zahra was cross and went to bed.

"PHEW". She heard Tommy's whistle.

She woke up and looked out of the window.

Magically, Santa and his reindeers were with
Tommy in the park and she ran to see them.

Santa hugged her and said,

"Your letter blew into my sleigh.

Guess what present I have brought you Zahra?"

And in Santa's sleigh was her Daddy.

She hugged Daddy very tightly.

Zahra asked Santa to make Tommy's Christmas wish come true.

Flying back to the North Pole Santa puzzled.
"How on earth can I do that?"

Then he shouted. "Ho Ho, Ho! I know how.

Mrs Claus and my breakfast must wait.
Rudolf, turn around. We are heading South!"

Zahra and her family spent Christmas Day together.

Mum and Dad saw Zahra on television and were very proud.

Even her grumpy brother said.

'I'm sorry Zahra for not believing you.'

Zahra, her brother and Daddy played football in the park.

"PHEW!" They heard Tommy's whistle again.

Tommy was awake and wanted to play football.

And he scored the goal to win the game

Then a young woman and a very old lady
came towards them.

Tommy went back to sleep...
people could not see him alive.

The young lady was Kate, the Princess of Wales.

She said,
"Santa came down Buckingham Palace chimney.
He told us Tommy's Christmas Wish
was to see his granddaughter.

We have found her and here she is."

The very old lady was Tommy's granddaughter, Edith. and Edith placed a red poppy at her grandfather's feet.

Everyone left Zahra alone with the sleeping Tommy.

She whispered, "Thank you Tommy, for bringing my Daddy home."

Suddenly, Edith's poppy blew up into the wind.

Magically, it fell into Zahra's hand.

Tommy woke up smiling and said,

"Keep my Edith's poppy safe and never forget those who died to keep you safe."

Tommy closed his eyes for the last time and he whispered, "Thank you for Edith, my own Christmas Wish.

Goodbye, Zahra."

Zahra danced home singing her metal friend's song.

Silent Night, Holy Night
Sleep in Heavenly Peace

THE END

APS Books
www.andrewsparke.com

First published worldwide by APS Books in 2022

WHY NOT GO AND SEE THE PLAYERS IN THIS STORY?

The metal sculpture of 'Tommy' was made by famous North East England artist Ray Lonsdale. Tommy sits every day in the park at Seaham Harbour , County Durham, England on the cliff tops overlooking the scene of the sea rescue. Opposite are the street and the shops where Zahra lived.

Ray also made 'The Coxswain', the sculpture of the lifeboat captain who brings the George Elmy lifeboat to help save the shipwrecked sailors. Both are located in Seaham.

The Brothers – waiting t' gan down' is a sculpture by Brian Brown which is also at Seaham Harbour and is a memorial to those pitmen who worked underground and under the sea in the three Seaham coal mines.

Santa of course is at the North Pole with all his reindeers.

And the Princess? ...well you know where she lives I'm sure

Printed in Great Britain
by Amazon

26931385R00016